Picasso's Piebald Perspectives

(the pony, that is, not the artist)

Vol 2

Brief Encanter

Ruth Whittaker

Grosvenor House
Publishing Limited

All rights reserved
Copyright © Ruth Whittaker, 2024

The right of Ruth Whittaker to be identified as the author of this
work has been asserted in accordance with Section 78
of the Copyright, Designs and Patents Act 1988

The book cover is copyright to Ruth Whittaker

This book is published by
Grosvenor House Publishing Ltd
Link House
140 The Broadway, Tolworth, Surrey, KT6 7HT.
www.grosvenorhousepublishing.co.uk

This book is sold subject to the conditions that it shall not, by way of
trade or otherwise, be lent, resold, hired out or otherwise circulated
without the author's or publisher's prior consent in any form of
binding or cover other than that in which it is published and
without a similar condition including this condition being
imposed on the subsequent purchaser.

This book is a work of fiction although the story
is based on real creatures, people and events.

A CIP record for this book
is available from the British Library

ISBN 978-1-83615-041-1

To John, for buying Picasso for me, and
the NHS, who enabled me to keep riding her.

Contents

Foreword – Deirdre Mackay, 2024 vii

Preface ix

Acknowledgments xi

1. Picasso Ponders 1
2. Picasso's Odyssey 6
3. Picasso in Pensive Mood 15
4. Peppermints 17
5. Perishing Picasso Here 18
6. Picasso Paddles 19
7. Paradisiacal Picasso 20
8. Plaintive Picasso 22
9. Picasso's Predicament 25
10. Prodigal Picasso? 27
11. Picture Perfect Picasso Today 29
12. Picasso's Odyssey Continues 30

13. Picasso Plodding 33

14. Peevish Picasso 35

15. Puggled Picasso 38

16. Pally Picasso 40

17. Perspiring Picasso 42

18. Primping Picasso 45

19. Party-mannered Picasso 46

20. Playful Picasso 48

21. Placatory Picasso 49

22. Placatory Picasso contd 51

23. Pensive Picasso 53

24. Peering Picasso 55

25. Picasso's Depilating 56

26. Praiseworthy Picasso 57

27. Picasso's Pronouncement 59

28. Picasso's Pleasure (and Pain) 61

29. Peripatetic Picasso 65

30. Picasso's Parting 68

Foreword

During my time as a local councillor I was privileged to meet many interesting and talented people. Amongst these people are Ruth and her late husband John. Not only is Ruth a talented writer, but she is also a gifted musician whose commitment to music is matched by her love of animals. It was here that I had my introduction to a haughty, piebald pony named Picasso.

Now, and I apologise to all the horse lovers out there, to me a horse used simply to be an animal with four legs, a long nose, long tail and a mane along its back. No more. I certainly had never 'met' a horse with an impressive following on Facebook.

So here is where Picasso came in; in this case a woman's best friend (and occasionally her foe) is unequivocally her pony. Picasso, due to her illustrious namesake, has an extraordinary talent for influencing humans, especially Ruth, into getting her own way and involving them in various scrapes along the way. Applying artistic flair as best she can, Picasso's approach to life is, by necessity, often deeply philosophical and frequently quite surreal. Rather than being led by the reins, this equine regularly reins in hapless bi-peds with an application of radical ideas and sheer strong will, often resulting in hilarious consequences.

Like many of you, I thoroughly enjoyed Ruth's first book, "Picasso's Piebald Perspectives', and have eagerly awaited this next chapter in her life which explores her relationship with Ollie. Now Ollie belongs to Ruth's granddaughter and is a very sporty chap with an engaging personality and impish sense of humour. He and Picasso quickly forge a strong bond.

I will leave you with this thought before you turn the page. Will this be the equine version of 'When Harry Met Sally"? Or, a bit like her namesake, will their journey be 'complicated'?

Deirdre Mackay 2024

Deirdre Mackay represented the ward of East Sutherland on The Highland Council from 2003 until 2022. She continues to live in the area, now able to devote more time to her love of gardening.

Preface

This isn't a book for exclusively 'horsey' types. Not in the least. It's for those who can appreciate life, seasoned with occasional romance, seen through the sardonic eyes of Willows Picasso, a black and white Gypsy Cob pony mare, whose two-leg I am.

Picasso IS female, to be clear. I didn't choose her name, and as it's considered bad form to change it, I haven't. Her eyes don't match. That on her right is normal horsey brown, while her left is disconcertingly azure. No-one's perfect. Nonetheless, Picasso's baleful gaze misses very little, from the ineptitude of her enthusiastic if decrepit two-leg (still nursing distant memories of nerveless pony-mad teens) to the approach of tit-bits.

In this collection of reflections, Picasso recounts her first meeting with White Eye aka Ollie aka Bryn Heulog Popalong, and how the pair were destined to be separated then reunited, several times over a decade. Poignantly emotional, in the tradition of iconic 1945 film, 'Brief Encounter'. For best effect, read to background music of Rachmaninov's 2nd Piano Concerto.

Acknowledgements

Ailsa Skirving-Carrick, the only girl in our year who wasn't terrified of our irascible art teacher at Jordanhill College School, for her wonderful illustrations.

Anne White, saddle fitter.

Diane Mackay, Doll Riding Centre, for instruction, support and guidance through UHI Level 6.

Derek Gill, astounding loser (he knows what I mean!) for his creativity and technical brilliance in devising the front cover.

Kessock Equine Vets, for routine interventions, less routine interventions and resultant invoices.

Kirsteen Mackintosh, Star Stables, for helping me regain my confidence after an accident, stabling and schooling Picasso.

Linda Gill, Derek's wife, for unwavering support, advice and dog-sitting.

Lorna Jappy, for always coaxing Picasso into the trailer, gophering at events and believing us unstoppable.

Lucy and Tommy, Shore Street Garage, Helmsdale, for trying valiantly to keep the old horse box on the road, then providing something with which to tow the new trailer.

Natalie Vincent, Pottofields Equestrian, for backing Picasso, and much more in the years to come.

Nicole Hawker, for trimming Picasso's hooves regularly.

NHS Highland Raigmore, Orthopaedic department, for bolting up a piece of my femur loosened in action.

Rebecca Dickie, my daughter, for sourcing Picasso in the first place.

1. Picasso Ponders

My winter coats come and go, but apart from that I don't change. However, I have experienced some noteworthy events over the seasons. Many winter coats ago, I was moved from where I was foaled, to Natalie, who first sat on my back, and made me go, and do, what she asked of me, when she asked. There were a few of my kind

there, but no-one of any interest, except a rather cheeky bay-coloured boy, who wasn't even as big as me.

"Ho ho ho! You're new round here! Just letting you know that I'm in charge!"

I ignored him, knowing perfectly well that this is how established residents greet newcomers. Especially how rather undersized established boy residents do it.

"You're a bit weird, aren't you?" he continued, strolling around me, trying to look important. I remained silent, looking down on him.

"I mean, one of your eyes is BLUE!"

Finally stung, I returned, "You're a fine one to talk! One of YOUR eyes is...well, I don't know what it is. Never seen anything like it in my life!"

The boy swished his tail. "It wasn't always like that, so there!"

"Oh? What happened?"

"Something sharp scratched it in a field, and then it went like this. I can't see out of it anymore, but it doesn't matter, 'cos I'm brilliant at jumping over stuff!"

"Really?" I replied. (A handy response expressing both sympathy over the injured eye, and disdain at his boastfulness.)

"Yes! You'll see me at it soon - I'm amazing!"

"Why would you want to jump over stuff anyway?"

"Dunno.....oh, I suppose I just do it 'cos the two-legs make me, and it makes them so happy that I get treats."

I understood the last bit, of course.

"What are you amazing at?" he continued. I confessed I didn't know yet.

Later on, I watched as two-legs caught the boy, decked him out in all the stuff they need, then one of them jumped aboard. In the next field, there were lots of objects lying around. The bay boy broke into a very orderly canter, and set off towards a heap of coloured sticks. I expected him to stop, or go around the side, for it seemed quite a bulky pile, but no - gathering his hooves under him, he popped neatly up and over, and cantered on, obviously happily, towards the next challenge, which he overcame with the same ease. I was extremely puzzled about the entire activity, but had little time to think about it, as I was immediately put into basic training by Natalie, which was rather hard work.

"Ho ho ho! Did you see me? Aren't I awesome?" demanded the boy, later.

"H'm. I think you're quite brave, but I don't fancy that sort of thing, personally."

Worryingly, it soon turned out that I too was expected to have a try at tackling the obstacles. I dutifully cantered up to the pile of sticks I was pointed at, and to avoid unnecessary effort, ran round the side of them. The two-leg sitting on my back wasn't pleased, however, turned me around and headed me for it again, also administering a smack to my rear with a stinging thing. With nothing else for it, I tried to do what I'd seen the bay boy do. Unfortunately, I rather muddled my legs, and ploughed through the thing, sending sticks flying. My rider next made me walk, then trot over other bits and pieces lying on the ground, before turning me out again, to think things over.

"You were rubbish!" commented the bay boy. Despondently, I had to agree.

"Never mind." he continued, cheerfully, "You're very pretty, so it won't matter if you can't jump much!"

"Do you think so?" I was worried about my future, not my looks.

"Oh yes. You'll do quite well in those games where we all walk around, and a prize goes to the nicest-looking. I don't do so well there, 'cos of my eye." he added, candidly.

"Well," I suddenly decided, "I think you're very nice looking anyway, and you're really clever." Always best to be generous, and it was truthful.

"Know what? - I'm going to call you 'Blue Eye'!" he announced.

I thought for a moment. "And I'll call you 'White Eye'!"

That was how we gave each other our names.

White Eye and I spent some time together, becoming good pals. White Eye went off one day, all washed and brushed, looking very smart, and when he returned much later, everyone was very pleased with him.

"I was the very best jumper today!" (he wasn't at all shy) "and the two-legs were given lots of coloured things to hang on my head!"

"Nice work!" I was impressed.

Soon after, sadly for our friendship, I was loaded into a huge moving thing, and taken away from both Natalie and White-Eye, to begin my life with HER. As I have already told you about those early days in my first volume of memoirs, I shall now continue from where I left off there.

2. Picasso's Odyssey

SHE came into our field, in that white thing that can move quickly on the roads, which is a sign that SHE's bringing quite a bit of equipment. First of all, SHE put out two bowls of breakfast, one each for Vala (my dismal companion) and me. SHE always puts Vala's far away from mine, to minimise hassle. Next, SHE turned HER attention to me, strapping those long boots on my legs, and that other thing around my tail. SHE was in a very happy frame of mind, indicating that SHE and I were about to do something really fun. Just at that point, my idiot companion, who's so possessive of HER, decided that I was monopolising too much of HER time, and charged to chase me away. I assure you that it's most upsetting, especially at breakfast time, and I plunged away at top speed, Vala snorting threats as she pursued me, ears back and teeth bared for action. Neither of us noticed HER for a moment or so, then I realised that SHE was lying on the ground, making an awful, distressed sort of noise. We both knew SHE was badly hurt.

"SHE'LL die!" quavered Vala.

"If SHE does, it'll be your fault!" I returned, more frightened, for once, by HER distress than by Vala's aggression.

Just then, two strange two-legs who'd happened to be passing, jumped over the fence, and ran to HER. After a little while, as we stood helplessly watching, they were able to make HER stand up, and SHE soon waved them away, going to sit in HER transport for a bit.

"SHE'S lamed." we both said.

'It's your fault!" we both added.

Slowly, SHE limped back to us. We realised that SHE wanted me to come out of our area, and that Vala was to stay. Very unsettled by the turn of events, we did what SHE wanted, and I waited for whatever was to come next. Very soon, a big moving stable, like the one which had brought me here, arrived and stopped by our field. Two more two-legs came out and whickered around with HER, before one took my lead rope, and between them coaxed me reluctantly up the ramp and into the thing. Turning my head, I called for HER. I don't like these stables very much, even less so when SHE's not around. SHE called something back in a nice soothing tone, so I thought I'd see HER again soon. The new two-legs closed up the box, and it set off jolting down the road. Vala shrieked hysterically after me, until I couldn't hear her any more.

SHE had given me lots of hay, and I could smell all my usual accessories, stowed away overhead. I stood and stood for a very very long time, until my box stopped at a strange place, frightening me with the noise of huge things going back and forth, hoards of two-legs hurrying around, and very unpleasant odours. The pair of two-legs were very kind, and reassured that I wouldn't be harmed, I followed them out of the box, into another where they gave me more hay, patted me and said goodbye. I called to them to come back, but they took no notice.

I thought I would die of terror at what happened next; my stable was suddenly lifted up, then pulled along and down into a frightful cavern with all sorts of glaring, flashing lights. The noise was dreadful - I jumped every time huge nearby objects clanged together, and two-legs shouted incomprehensible stuff at each other. Over somewhere to one side, I heard some meat-eaters howling dismally for their two-legs, and began to fear the worst. Gradually however, the noise and bustle subsided, and another two-leg came to give me water. He patted me kindly, but went away again. Next, the entire vast cavern was suddenly plunged into darkness. A new noise began to throb through the place, and I could feel everything moving in a strange way. I was very tired, and would have liked to lie down, but although there was room to do so, and comfortable bedding beneath me, my stable would move down to one side, then back up again, so I thought it best to try to stand straight. Once or twice, I was almost unbalanced by the movement of this box, but agreed with myself that in fact, nothing seemed to want to harm me. I wondered about HER. SHE had been very lame.

After a very long time, swaying from side to side in this dark place, the background noise changed, lights flashed into life, and I felt a bump as the whole place came to a standstill. Two-legs reappeared, shouting to each other above the noise of things being started up. Further along, a great door slowly opened, and I could see daylight outside. Something took hold of my stable box again, and hauled it outside into the sunshine. I was extremely glad to be out of that horrible dark, noisy, swaying place, but now anxious about what would happen to me next.

"Hello Picasso!" Several voices were calling me. I craned my neck to see, and recognised HER offspring and a grand foal, which was a huge relief, believe me. After some more jolting around, another two-leg opened my stable and led me out. I felt oddly unsteady, but hurried away from it towards the treat HER offspring was holding. I wasn't too pleased at having to clamber into yet another box, but at least it was of a type I'm quite used to, so decided to settle down with a fresh hay net for the next leg.

I was amazed, when yet again, I could feel that swaying sensation. What was wrong with the ground here to make it move like that? I decided that I didn't want the hay anymore, and dearly longed to get outside on my own again. At long last, the box stopped, and I was led out into a field, where HER family patted me, and turned me loose to roll and stretch my tired legs.

A thunder of approaching hooves told me that some of my kind were coming to inspect. In fact, there was quite a herd - a big girl, a tiny black and white girl, a young girl with her she-foal, and a smallish bay boy. The big girl blew on me disdainfully and turned away. The foal came bounding over asking me to play with her, while her mother threatened me with death. I ignored that, gaining approval from the tiny black and white girl.

"She's crazy," she remarked, 'too young to cope with a foal. Take no notice."

I thought she was very wise, probably because she was also very old.

The boy, meantime, had been walking round me, head on one side, taking stock.

"Blue Eye? Blue Eye - is it you?"

With a sigh of relief, I recognised my old mucker, White Eye from Natalie's place, so many winter coats ago. We'd become friends after making fun of each other's eyes - one of mine is blue, they say, and one of his is white all over. He can't see with that eye, but it never bothered him a bit. I was learning to carry a two-leg, and he was doing lots of jumping over things. After work, we used to spend time together, sometimes having a race, sometimes standing head to tail, flicking flies off each other. I was delighted to find him here. I told him about my horrible experience in the swaying darkness, and he explained that sometimes two-legs move on the top of water, which accounts for the strange motion.

"They do it a lot here," adding, "you'll see."

"Look at me, I can kick up my heels!" cried the foal, barging cheekily past us. She was a pretty little thing, though her mother ought to have told her not to annoy her elders.

"Needs a nip." White Eye remarked. "Her mother's hopeless, though."

I agreed, and we ambled away to a quiet corner for a catch-up. White Eye belongs to the smallest two-leg, and when she calls "Ollie!", he knows he's wanted.

White Eye told me that after leaving Natalie, he travelled for a very long time, also over water, to a herd of two-legs who were very kind to him, but very firm in expecting him to do his best when taken to events where he had to jump over lots of obstacles.

"I AM very good at it," he admitted, modestly, "but only if my two-leg asks me correctly."

"What do you do if you haven't been asked correctly?"

"Either I run out by the side, or stop dead and watch 'em fly off over my shoulder!"

He snorted in happy recall of ejecting inept two-legs. I was impressed, and twitched my ears for the rest of his story.

"I stayed there for a long time, but I realised that the small two-leg who rode me was growing bigger and heavier, until one day I was loaded into the trailer, without all the usual preparations for an event. My two-leg was terribly unhappy, and hugged me tightly, making me realise that I was going away from her for good. I was sad too, but after a long time, crossing water several times, I arrived here. These two-legs are very kind too, though my new rider still has a bit to learn. Sometimes I'll help her out, if I'm feeling tolerant. I do realise that it's important for them to be given those coloured things that hang from our bridles, so I know what to do, when push comes to shove. What about you, Blue Eye? Natalie was very pleased with you, and you were always so well-behaved."

I told White Eye about HER, how SHE isn't in the least like Natalie, though always very kind and considerate. SHE doesn't know how to get me really moving when I don't want to, but as this doesn't seem to be much of a problem for HER, I just potter along.

"SHE did make me jump a couple of times, but although I quite enjoy it, I'm not very good. - I still tend to get my hooves muddled up!" I confessed.

"Well, we can't all be good at this," said White Eye, generously, 'but on the other hand, you ARE very pretty!"

"I know." He was correct, after all. "SHE does take me to these events where you amble round and round with a small herd, then have to trot behind HER. I'm always given a coloured thing, and then SHE always rubs HER muzzle against me, which is disgusting!"

"Sounds rather tame." White Eye sounded critical. 'Any companions?"

"Only a bullying neurotic, who thinks she has to protect HER from me. In fact, it was because I was escaping from this stupid girl, that I accidentally brushed past HER…quite hard, I suppose….and knocked HER over…then SHE went very lame."

"Serious. Has SHE sent you away because of that?"

"I don't know. SHE wasn't cross with me." Just the same, it occurred to me that maybe I had been sent away by myself for hurting HER.

"Can't be helped anyway. C'mon, I'll show you around."

Fresh fields, with a vengeance.

3. Picasso in Pensive Mood

As you may imagine, HER grand foals are keeping my nose to the grindstone. Out and about almost every hour of daylight, with my old mucker, White Eye. They call him "Ollie". I'm quite happy here with all of them, though I don't entirely share their work ethic. White Eye's taken to showing a bit of attitude with the smaller grand foal - you know the sort of thing - perversely heading in the opposite direction, punctuated by a few bullying little bucks, which worry her. The older grand foal has taken to dealing with him, putting her younger sibling up on me. White Eye keeps inciting me to behave like him, but I'm disinclined to start the day so energetically. I irritate my small rider by standing stock still - so much less effortful. She's too small to leg me on effectively, but once bored, I heave a sigh and trudge out. After this swap, White Eye behaves himself, so then, just to show esprit de corps, I put in a few bucks. Just enough to enliven rather than petrify, you understand. I also think I'm getting the hang of this jumping lark, yet acknowledge that White Eye's king in this respect.

I do return to wondering about HER. While White Eye's used to tearing around courses crammed with jumpable objects, SHE and I used to enjoy moderate success in beauty contests. I knew when one of these was in the offing, through being caught up and put through the most disconcerting routine of reluctant bathing and general titivating within an inch of my life. Inevitably, this culminated in processing round and round in the company of similarly tarted-up examples of our kind, sometimes trotting, sometimes being asked to canter (I always draw the line here, on principle) until we're called in to receive small flappy things which evidently delight our two-legs. I've come to recognise several of my fellow-kind on these jaunts. One girl's a bit bigger than me, and seems to be the sector leader. She told me that she was the best anyway, and that my eyes were odd. I told her that my eyes (which White Eye likes, 'cos they're unusual - one brown, one blue) were well up to observing that unlike me, she has the head of a dray horse. Honesty is always the best policy.

On reflection, I rather miss these outings, bathing aside. SHE always lavished edible encouragements, and substantial numbers of HER two-leg friends would amble up to make a fuss of both of us. -And I didn't have to heave myself over obstacles at speed. Wish SHE'd come and see me.

4. Peppermints

Picasso loves them. Accepted them with alacrity, as is my due, from HER. Dunno where SHE's been, but who cares? I see that SHE's definitely not going sound, and seems to have grown another pair of leg-things for support. SHE is here now, and has peppermints. White Eye, the bigger girl, and the cheeky foal all suddenly arrived, lured by the irresistible aroma, and all unfortunately enjoyed some from HER, which ought to have been exclusively reserved for me. Better little than nothing, I suppose. Before I could say "more", HER grand foal was out again, saddling and harassing me, furthermore, with a stick which SHE'd bought her. I may waste away.

5. Perishing Picasso Here

Chivvied far and away beyond the call of duty by the two grand foals.

Hassled uphill, downhill, over the sticks this way, then back that way, occasionally receiving an intensely irritating tap on my pelt like a fly landing, from the smaller rider. Have exercised extreme restraint.

At one point, SHE called to me, from a conveyance in the field, and I was quite glad to amble over and accept compliments and a peppermint from HER. SHE thoughtlessly left a sliver of silver paper on the treat, but beggars frankly can't be choosers. Anyway, it's so so cold here, I'll probably freeze to death before suffering any harm from a scrap of foil.

"Give her a bad time!" suggested White Eye wickedly, running out neatly at the last minute from a set of poles he could've stepped over. He loses interest rapidly unless challenged, bless him. I knew what he meant, but Better Feelings towards my small jockey sort of won the day.

I just wish it was warmer.

6. Picasso Paddles

All new and puzzling, to begin with. I've never enjoyed water, except for drinking, and offered a certain resistance to going close to it, today. White Eye, however, plunged straight in, and called me a coloured coward, because he can be rather rude. There was nothing for it but to try the stuff gingerly, pawing each step to ensure that it was safe underfoot.

I wasn't impressed that SHE was watching and laughing at me, so I took my courage in all four hooves, and waded in, to universal cries of encouragement. In fact, once I was well and truly in the wet stuff, and had checked it for drinkability (unsuitable) it was quite pleasant, and my hooves felt quite refreshed.

SHE gave me a titbit afterwards. Glad SHE wasn't aboard, or I'd probably have sunk without trace

7. Paradisiacal Picasso

Is there anything more glorious than a satisfactory back-scratching session? Aaaaaah. Access all areas.

It's been tough. White-Eye/Ollie, my mini-mucker, is having a middle-aged crisis, I suspect. Loads of attitude, prancing around in the wrong direction, showing off in front of the other girls, usual stuff. During such episodes, I tend to switch off, and come to a grinding halt, which in turn impels the rider to flap her legs against my saddle, and wield that maddening stick. It's akin to being irritated by a colony of small ants. SHE hobbled up and gave me a ticking off, so I reluctantly plodded forth.

"Keep your capering backside out of my face!" I instructed, as White Eye performed an intimidating pirouette in reverse gear.

"I'll do as I please!" he sniggered.

'That's as may be, but if you stick your bum in my face again, I'll bite it."

"You wouldn't!"

'Try me, laddie."

HER offspring arrived, and taking firm hold of White Eye, led him back onto the straight and narrow. I sighed and fell into line, enduring more of the ant-stinging for a stroll down to the big watery place. Back at home base at last, there was nothing for it but to ease away all my irritations. Two-legs and showing off boys. Who needs 'em?

8. Plaintive Picasso

I hardly know what's going on. HER offspring caught me up, brushed me nicely, and loaded me into the moving stable. White Eye called, "Where are you going, Blue Eye? Can't I come too?"

Realising that I was going away on my own, I called back to him, 'I don't want to go without you, White Eye!" It was no use, and after a longish run, I was unloaded, then re-loaded into a cage thing, and taken into the huge noisy dark place that I now remembered from some time ago. The offspring had seemed sad, and it dawned on me that I was going far away again. I wasn't happy, still less as the huge dark place began to move under my hooves, and kept doing that for a long long time. Somewhere in the darkness, meat eaters howled miserably again, and those creatures that moo moo-ed disconsolately, from time to time. I felt quite bad, and couldn't lie down and rest comfortably. Eventually, as before, the movement stopped, lights blazed, and everything around became even noisier and busier. My box was hauled outside, where it was cooler, then I was unloaded and given to another two-leg. She was kind, and I remembered that she'd brought me here in the first place, some time ago. She loaded me into yet another moving stable, and offered me a drink and some hay, but I wasn't hungry. We set off. I didn't know what was going to happen to me. I was hot and sweaty, and felt very sorry for myself.

I knew that I wouldn't see White Eye and was all on my own. I thought back to when I used to live with HER and my neurotic companion, and felt even more sad. SHE was always very kind, and an ever-present source of food and treats. I wondered what had happened to HER.

Finally, the box came to a halt.

"Picasso!!"

It was - actually- HER!! I was so relieved, I was quite cross. Where had SHE been all this time? SHE offered me some treats, not half as quickly as SHE ought to have done, and removed my hot travel boots. Lots more of my kind gathered to call hello from a nearby field, so I cheered up immensely as kindly two-leg Kirsteen led me to a new field where three more of my kind waited. SHE watched me roll on my stiff muscles, and provided more treats. At last, SHE had to go, but I think SHE said SHE'd be back tomorrow. I should think so too.

9. Picasso's Predicament

To do, or not to do, that is the question.

Spent some time sorting out the pecking order. To my amusement, my field mates approached me, forming a deputation of three, led by the smallest.

"We feel we need to tell you that this is OUR space, and so..."

"Yes?" I turned my heels towards him, quietly but firmly.

"Oh...nothing, really.."

"No. The fact is that I shall do what I want, where I want here, and expect you pathetic runts to stay away. Understand?"

"Erm...that's what we thought." came the lame response. They'd have been much lamer if they'd persisted. Next, a new two-leg appeared, calling for me to go to her. I might've shambled over, but acutely aware of my watchful peers, and the importance of keeping up appearances, I stood my ground, obliging the two-leg to come to me. I was led away, slightly apprehensively, to one of those places where I've been put through my paces. The two-leg spent some time encouraging me to walk, trot, halt, turn and back up, whilst I pretended never to have been asked to do this sort of thing before. Then, shiver my withers, SHE tottered up, and made all sorts of positive noises. Soon I was led back to the yard, where the new two-leg groomed me (very competently, I noted) while talking to HER.

All very sociable, but I simply don't understand why I'm here, if SHE's around. It's not as if I need to be taught any manners.

10. Prodigal Picasso?

Can you just hear me rolling my eyes? After an astonishingly long time, when I've been trundled all over the world, and ridden by an assortment of two-legs, suddenly SHE wobbles back into my life.

I've been having a rather regimented time recently, being organised pleasantly but firmly by Kirsteen. Judge of my astonishment then, when I was brushed, saddled and led to the mounting block, to have HER hop aboard once more. I'd never really given this point much attention, but SHE is heavier than all recent two-legs. I'm merely making an observation - I can tote HER perfectly well, but if SHE cared to shed a few pounds, as I've been forced to…..just saying. Anyway, off we went with that snooty black girl, Eden.

"Get too close and I'll kick you." she sniffed.

"Darling, you're full of wind," I returned, jogging quickly alongside, "and I'm far more capable of delivering a meaningful kick, so let's just concentrate on entertaining the two-legs."

Eden swished her tail haughtily, but nevertheless took my advice, and shied at a bird, so I duly followed suit.

SHE was in no danger of coming unstuck, I discerned, nor did SHE shriek nor clutch at my reins. I then pretended to be about to bolt ahead, but strategies like this are unnecessarily effortful, and as SHE had passed my assessment of basic competence, I contented myself with striding out purposefully.

Back at the starting point, SHE exited her position, a tad stiffly I thought, then removed my tack and gave me a good all over brushing. I remembered that back at my old home with HER, Chuck and his fellow-flyers would've been busy at this time of year, collecting my redundant winter coat hairs. Once returned to my field, SHE removed my headcollar. Nary a miserable titbit? I was SO disappointed, and was about to turn away, when SHE put a fresh sliced carrot on the ground for me.

Changing times and habits.

11. Picture Perfect Picasso Today

Out for a look around this morning, with my new acquaintance, Eden. SHE tacked me up all by HERSELF this morning - I'd begun to wonder when SHE'd get around to this again. I stood very politely while SHE had a long chat with Kirsteen (whom, I have to admit, I'm quite fond of) then moved off obediently, just to show how biddable I can be.

Eden took it into her head to pretend to see predators lurking in the tufts of grass. This sort of thing's all very well, but can be irksome when (as I was) in a cooperative mindset. SHE's definitely beginning to remember what to do and urged me firmly on, when I briefly tested HER resolve, passing that certain shed on Kirsteen's drive. I therefore decided to be sanctimonious, even taking the lead a couple off times, when Eden pulled that old, "I-won't-pass-by-that-and-you-can't-make-me" ploy. The morning was pleasant, and I was happy to jog along, enjoying the sights and sounds. The contrast in our attitudes couldn't have been more marked; me, relaxed and positive, Eden on the alert for the next terror waiting to pounce from her over-active imagination. I, of course, am always sensible and compliant. Unless I'm not.

12. Picasso's Odyssey Continues

I was having a chat with my new little friend, Blue. I don't often bother to be friends with those who share my field, but Blue was a bit special, being very quiet and respectful. I sensed that he wasn't perhaps in the best of health and strength, although he was always cheerful, and - he was the first boy since White Eye to notice that I was pretty. He didn't want to run around like an idiot, kicking up his heels and blowing off odorous wind for no reason at all, as the others seemed to, so we took to grazing together, and discussing the usual topics of food and two-legs.

He explained that he had been in a very bad place before coming here, without enough to eat and drink. He was very happy now, of course, with lots of two-legs to care for him, but told me that nobody ever rode on him. We did out best to groom each other, cleaning off our winter coats, though Blue couldn't quite reach up to my back.

"Sorry." he said, "I'm not much good am I?"

"Oh that's alright - I can always have a good roll and scratch."

'Just mind my neck - your teeth are sharp."

"Sorry." I apologised in turn.

SHE turned up, plus a two-leg companion whom I realised I'd met before, way back when I used to live close to HER. SHE caught me, and started to lead me out of the field.

"Goodbye." said little Blue, quietly. He's always quiet, though.

"I'll see you in a little while, once SHE's finished jogging me around the block."

"No. You're going away. I hope you have a lovely time."

I followed HER, suddenly uneasy, to that moving stable SHE has, which, I remembered, I don't like. I looked back at Blue, standing where I had left him, and decided that I didn't want to go away somewhere else, yet again, and firmly refused to follow HER up the ramp. After a few futile attempts to dupe me, HER friend took my rope. I thought for a few seconds, then sighing, followed the apple up and into the box. There was hay there too, so I munched, pooped and resigned myself to my fate.

After being joggled about for a shortish time, the box stopped, and the two-legs untied me, and allowed me to pick my way down into a very nicely green field. As SHE unfastened those hot travel boots, I realised that I was, well - HOME. It felt a bit strange somehow, but there was plenty of grass. Blue would've liked to come with me, I thought, missing him rather.

SHE put me in through a new gate. Odd. Same field, but different posts and things. I trotted off to examine the boundaries. One of those fences that smacks you if you touch it. Then it dawned on me that I was on my own, apart from HER and HER companion. I remembered that I used to have a companion here, neurotic idiot that she was, but no longer. My kind knows when one of us has gone forever, however, so I accepted that. I just wonder though, if I'm really home for good? I've met lots of my kind while I've been away, and lots of kindly two-legs, but none of them were MY two-leg. SHE's been back to see me, and offered more carrot, but when there's some lovely fresh grass - maybe, just maybe, there's no place like Home?

13. Picasso Plodding

Uphill. It sank in that I was really and truly back at my own home, today. SHE staggered down to my field, laden with my tack. Frankly, I was glad to see HER, for it was a pleasant morning, and I wanted a change of scene. SHE led me out, and tied me up beside a hay net, but there was so much scrumptious fresh new grass, that I couldn't be bothered with the hay. SHE struggled to fasten my girth, eventually managing, practically strangling me in the process. Next, SHE led me away along the road, and down the steep hill towards the other fields I've sometimes been in. I was entirely happy to amble along behind HER, though I began to wonder if SHE intended to ride me. We arrived, however, at the place where SHE used to clamber aboard, so I duly lowered my head to hoover up some more lovely grass, while SHE took up position, asking me to walk on. I'd had a fun time while staying with HER grand foals, utterly refusing to walk on, if no authoritative two-leg was around, so decided to try that joke. SHE wasn't amused, applying HER heels firmly to my flanks. I'd noted SHE carried a stick too. SHE's probably afraid to use it, but one never knows. Why court trouble?

We walked on, therefore, past a couple of worrying objects, then set off up another hill. Goodness, I'd forgotten just how steep these hills are, and fairly soon, I was slightly sweaty and slightly, only slightly, out of breath. SHE didn't push me hard, but wouldn't let me stop either, so I kept going until one of those horrid horned brown beasts suddenly leaped out of a whin bush and bounded away, while I jumped, startled. SHE soothed me, and on we plodded, finally reaching the top of the hill. SHE talked away to me, in that inane way SHE has, until we reached the last corner before home. There was a most unsettling new confrontation, in the form of a row of tubs big enough for me to drink from, filled with lots of coloured things swaying around in the sea breeze. I didn't want to pass them, and did a little protest dance to affirm this. I sensed that SHE was uneasy, but SHE kept talking to me, and squeezing me with those heels of HERS, until I took a brave sideways scuttle past those things, snorting concern for my safety. SHE rewarded me with effusive praise, and posted a piece of carrot forward, for my bravery. I see that nothing has changed, in that SHE's amazingly courageous about things that absolutely petrify me, yet anxious about something(s) that I can neither see nor hear. Two-legs are odd.

14. Peevish Picasso

I know that there's a sizeable carrot lying out there beside my tack. SHE's not given it to me, so I'm having to content myself with some more hay. SHE wouldn't even let me snatch some luscious new grass, after releasing me from that saddle. Another thing, SHE made me trot uphill for quite a bit, which became effortful - equally for HER, so we're quits.

What's got into HER, regarding that carrot? We set off in fine style. SHE'd given me a lovely brushing, which is great right now, when I'm shedding the last of my winter coat, and we both knew how smart I looked. Along the road, then down the steep hill. SHE never hustles me, allowing me to pick my way carefully. We passed the bleaters and their young, then, because I'd had enough, I decided to turn around, gently but firmly, for home. SHE apparently had other ideas, and turned me round again, urging me forward. I was displeased, and tried to turn again, but SHE repeated her tactic. This was rather annoying, so I decided to go backwards along the grassy path we sometimes have a little canter along. SHE seemed very worried about this, and turned me again, so's I couldn't go back. By this time, I was thoroughly annoyed with

HER unreasonable attitude, so stood stock-still, refusing to go forward. We repeated the whole pointless manoeuvre several times, always returning to my halt position. I did NOT want to go on, and I could tell from HER voice that SHE did. Next, I felt a slight but focussed stinging and realised that SHE had actually applied the whip SHE always carries as an ornament. There followed several more rotations, then just as I was becoming dizzy and might well have thrown in the towel, SHE struggled down off my back, ran up my stirrups, and taking the reins over my head, proceeded to lead me on down the hill. I could of course have been really firm, pulled my head away and headed for home on my own, but in a spirit of forgiveness, followed HER meekly, stopping, starting and backing as instructed by HER. Then, we arrived at one of HER companion's place. Hearing HER call, the companion (whom I know to be rather too knowledgeable for my comfort) held my head, giving me to understand that under no circumstances should I attempt a sideways jig, while SHE re-mounted. Back on course, SHE seemed frankly vindictive, urging me into a reluctant trot, which pace SHE maintained for as long as SHE could, past our first halting place, until we were pointing firmly for home. Unfortunately, we had several more clashes of wills, as I refused to go in any other direction but homewards, even for a couple of steps, finally winning, as SHE returned me to my field, after lifting my hooves to check for foreign bodies, and all that fuss, but - not a single carrot!

So, I am here, and the carrot, I can smell, is over there. I can just imagine that if SHE leaves it, Chuck, of one of his flying relatives, will swoop down and filch it. How could SHE be so mean to me? What have I done to deserve it?

15. Puggled Picasso

SHE hove in sight, with a new companion two-leg. I allowed myself to be caught, natch, and pulled methodically at my hay net, whilst they brushed me, picked my hooves and tacked me up. I had a neat trick ready, namely blowing myself up with air to make it pretty difficult to fasten my saddle. SHE, however, has found some accessory or other that overcomes the problem. Win some, lose some.

So, firmly on course for another victory, I stood politely while HER new companion (NC hereinafter) parked herself atop me. SHE walked alongside, whickering amicably away to HER NC, whilst I plodded obligingly ....until we reached the start of the downhill, where I, already bored, stopped. The NC applied rather authoritative legs, though I chose to ignore them. Next, however, the NC took HER ornamental whip, and delivered me several stinging smacks, very firm legs, and a vocal tone I interpreted as distinctly unamused. I shuffled off, receiving praise, which was actually mortifying.

You have no idea, none whatsoever, of what followed. Under no circumstances did NC allow me to stop when I wanted to. Furthermore, I was made to stop when I didn't want to. SHE did HER pathetic best to keep up - and I confess I kept a slightly anxious ear out for Her, as NC bid fair to debar me for ever from my comfort zone. It dawned on me that it'd be easier for me to pretend to comply. In consequence, NC only allowed me my favourite canter after I'd done lots of stops/starts/turns to her satisfaction. I had to do an odd sideways manoeuvre, until NC was pleased with me, and all in all by the time we arrived back at home base, I was quite ready to call it a day. No such luck though, as in spite of my protests, NC made me go on past my field, and away along the road again. I was relieved that SHE walked alongside, and eventually NC swung down off my back, leading me to a knoll where SHE could clamber aboard again. I did my best to waltz around, making it tricky for the old bat, but blow me if NC didn't reset me firmly. I relaxed as SHE took HER rickety place in the saddle, correctly assessing that nothing complex would be asked thereafter. Nonetheless, I was required to act against my better judgement, as NC insisted that SHE ride me back and forward several times past those frightening things by the house along the road. I did accrue carrots and masses of praise, but it was a harrowing hack. Could it be that the two-legs are conspiring to prune my individuality?

16. Pally Picasso

Sometimes life seems very good. This morning, SHE rolled down, clearly intent on business, but although I thanked HER in anticipation, SHE didn't immediately give me my start of the day treat. I had to content myself with a friendly pat, which is as much use as an empty hay net. Still, always interested in, and supportive of, HER various effortful activities, I watched while SHE found the thing that collects my poop, and began to fill it with odds and ends that have been left lying around - not by HER - and, I know, are irritating HER. I have become accustomed to hearing HER sometimes addressing something that isn't there. I know when SHE's talking to me, other two-legs, HER meat-eaters, or even Chuck and his flying family, but sometimes SHE speaks crossly to - well, nothing. This morning was a fine example, as SHE tugged a couple of things out of my stable, and took them to the poop-collector, finally trundling the load up and out of the field, soliloquising the while.

I whinnied approval as SHE returned, unloaded and finally rewarded my loyalty with a couple of treatlets, before bringing my hay. Beyond doubt, HER mood had lifted, and after SHE'd poop-picked and changed my water, SHE set-to with those brushes to help me shed my vestigial winter coat.

In the final analysis, there's little to beat munching a tranquil breakfast under warm sunshine (it's been depressingly wet until recently) while SHE brushes me. SHE has many weaknesses, but brushing isn't one, so I stood contentedly while SHE removed itchy loose hair from the middle of my back, where I can't reach it myself, took a scratchy twig out of my tail, and brushed off dried mud from where I'd been lying down earlier. Chuck scanned the proceedings from nearby, glad of more of my hair for his place. At peace with the world, SHE finally sat down in front of me, and we had a quick chat.

SHE: "Rambleramblerambleramble, Picasso."

Me: "For goodness sake get up before you stiffen up."

17.   Perspiring Picasso

What a time of it I've had this morning. SHE rolled down, laden with - I had to pause to remember, as it's been so long - all the kit SHE needs to take me out and about. A juicy carrot proffered and accepted, I followed HER out to where oodles of grass waited to be trimmed by me. SHE gave me a swift brush-up, looked at my hooves, then with uncharacteristic briskness had my tack on and led me to the thing SHE needs to climb, before hoisting HERSELF aboard. I could see no reason to object, being a) rather bored with my field b) mildly concerned that SHE hadn't been quite HER usual self, so willing to buck HER up....metaphorically, of course. SHE couldn't buck up literally, as effectively as I.

To test HER resolve, I pretended not to want to move off, but without hesitation, SHE tapped me behind my saddle, so in utter shock, I shuffled off in first gear. More leg pressure followed, prompting me to behave and walk smartly ahead, to lots of approving sounds from the passenger deck. We encountered several two-legs, who correctly admired me, and sauntered on companionably, while SHE performed what I now recognise as our signature tune, in the faux-courageous way SHE has, after a period of absence from this activity. Unfortunately, our tranquility was shattered, when I saw a long yellow snake lying across the road. Worse yet, water was streaming from it, and try as SHE might, I couldn't be persuaded to go near it. I even offered to take a short cut, by jumping down a steep bank, but SHE wouldn't let me. Maybe just as well. Finally, SHE struggled down onto terra firma, and led me right up to the snake. I'm much braver when SHE goes first, as of course if the snake had seized HER, I could've made my escape. Anyway, though I was far from happy, SHE insisted that I follow HER, then - believe it or not - SHE picked up a length of the snake, and held it out to me!!! I snorted anxiously, longing to flee, yet also anxious not to be shown up by a puny two-leg. SHE actually coiled the snake, and shook it around in front of me, until I was finally assured of its harmlessness. I breathed hard for a few steps until distracted by pats and more carrot.

We walked home, for which I was glad, as I was very hot and bothered by then, and SHE rubbed me down and turned me out. I was standing around, brain in neutral, when SHE produced the thing that fills my water bowl, clearly pointing it in my direction. The raw recollection of the yellow snake resurfaced to scare me, to the extent that I moved a few steps away from my hay, but undeterred, SHE directed a trickle of water at my legs. Another memory came back to me, that SHE used to do this to cool me down after a sweaty stroll, so re-parked myself by the hay, while SHE sluiced off the stickiness, and scraped off the excess water with one of HER incomprehensible accessories. I discerned that SHE, too, was super-heated, and fully expected HER to souse HERSELF with the water-snake, but SHE didn't. Was I expected to do it for HER?

18. Primping Picasso

Why, SHE? Why are you doing all this stuff to me? I don't especially mind being bathed, as it's a warm afternoon. Furthermore, you're being more than usually generous with titbits and adulation. Nonetheless, I'm slightly concerned that such a baptism of oddly-scented products, and torrents of water, may compromise my protective layers.

Why is SHE huffing and puffing all over me? What can be afoot, or more appropriately, ahoof?

19. Party-mannered Picasso

I always admire my own cleverness. If, by some unfortunate quirk of fate I'd won my class, I'd have had to hang around this festival of my sort for many hours, until the Grand Parade. As it is, while red-rosetted poseurs and neurotics wait, becoming more fretful and intractable by the moment, I'm happily back home in my peaceful field.

I'd made up my mind to give HER and HER very helpful companion an easy time today. So, after the usual preliminaries, I plodded obediently around, in the company of two other girls, walking/trotting/halting/backing immediately on request. SHE, I could tell, was especially pleased by the way I matched my trot to her -now- slight lameness. Allowances must be made. A he-two-leg approached, looking me over in detail. Both SHE and I instinctively felt that he wasn't bowled over by me. No accounting for tastes. He actually opined, yes he did, that I was fat! SHE made a humble sounding response, and once he'd gone, scratched my ear. The other two girls were clearly career showring denizens, and spoke neither to each other, nor to me. SHE kept up a line of chatty incomprehensible with me, and after the critical two-leg had given HER a rosette,

SHE was in high good humour, planting a kiss on my muzzle. I wish SHE wouldn't do that. Anyway, thanks to my curvaceous looks, we were all safely back home in time for a sunny afternoon. I generally have the last laugh.

20. Playful Picasso

I have perfected a hilarious activity, called immobility. When amusing myself thus, I stand stock-still, refusing to budge an inch. I don't do it when SHE's walking alongside, as SHE was today, whilst I toted the youngest of HER two-leg family. I mean, I threatened to stop, but SHE addressed me in severe tones, even tapping me with that stick thing she has, so I agreed to continue on straight and level. The small two-leg was polite, and knew what to do, up there in the cockpit, which rendered active resistance fairly pointless. Back home (or so I thought) SHE decided to mount up. I took a couple of steps, then planted myself. Top Fun! SHE paddled around futilely with HER legs, finally begging the smaller two-leg to lead me on! Vantage Picasso!! Silly old relic had to endure the shame of being led by a small two-leg!

21. Placatory Picasso

It took me a little time to realise that something was amiss. It's that time, of course, when nights start to be colder and longer, grass frazzles, and I grow a thicker coat again. I recognise all these seasonal changes but did not at first spot the subtle change in HER.

SHE's continue to visit me daily, change my water bowl, pick my poop, give me a treat, attempt to pet me as always, but I have sensed that all was not well. Yesterday, SHE stood beside me, and while scratching the area of my back which I can't reach, spilled out a more-in-sorrow-than-in-anger saga, which I didn't fully grasp, though it referenced HER daily care of me in the context of my reciprocal obligation to HER. I listened for a few moments, then pottered off, bored. SHE completed the daily routine, then sloped off in unmistakeable dejection.

Struck by a thought, I stopped what I was doing - very little, as is my preferred default position. It's fortunate that our kind is well-endowed with our own brand of sense. Applying my own share of this to the situation, it dawned suddenly on me that SHE was saying a sad goodbye. I was shocked and cross all at once. How could SHE want to part with me? I walked up and down, ignoring the friendly overtures of the boy in the next field, as I applied my intellect to this worrying predicament. What would happen to me? Sent away again to strange two-legs? I shivered, thinking about some of the two-legs I'd seen at the events we'd taken part in. Pulling their mounts about, making them gallop around, walloping them with purposeful sticks - did I want to be used like that? No fear. I kept returning to the Why of this development. SHE thought I wasn't doing what was expected of me, self-centred two-leg that SHE was. I was indignant, telling myself that I never hurt HER. Time wore on, and I began to wonder if I could change her mind? What a worry.

22. Placatory Picasso contd....

Spotting HER striding purposefully down, I wisely put on a spurt, and was waiting, calling a cheery welcome. Thought it'd be a wise investment. SHE gave me the regulation treat, then led me to the hitching-post, where SHE groomed and tacked me up, whilst I tidied up some long grass. All set, SHE led me to the place where I've been having even more fun recently, swinging out of HER reach, as SHE tries to get aboard. As SHE took a firm grip, I did my neat swerve, leaving HER high and dry on the things SHE climbs upon. Immediately, SHE jumped down, led me around and back into position. In a flash of inspiration, I realised that SHE was totally lacking in a sense of humour, which was why SHE was seriously thinking of sending me away. Imitating those of our kind which I've seen, reduced to unquestioning servitude, I therefore stood immobile, enabling HER to take up her seat. Obedient then to HER firmer than usual commands, I set off politely, allowing HER to believe that SHE now had the upper hand. A model of deportment, I walked, trotted and halted on the instant, harvesting pathetically grateful thanks and appreciation.

Encountering one of HER companions, I permitted an affectionate pat, whilst SHE permitted me to sample some thistles. We wended our amicable way back home, where SHE removed my outerwear, and returned me to my field, plied with praise and treats. I felt fairly confident that by compliance, I'd turned the situation around in my favour once more, but to be on the safe side, I ambled alongside as SHE poop-picked, giving HER the odd gentle nudge with my muzzle, to cement my place in HER affections. As SHE gave me another irritating pat, and stood looking at me, I had the supreme inspiration. Stifling my distaste of fuss, and the smell of two-leg breath, I stretched my neck and brushed HER muzzle with mine. Notwithstanding the weld of disgust with hypocrisy which flooded my senses, I was also keenly aware of having successfully courted and regained HER affections, and called tender haste-ye-backs to HER departing figure. The end often justifies the means.

23. Pensive Picasso

Another winter coat's doing stalwart work repelling dreary, sleety rain. Been many changes to my routine since I shed last year's model. I left the place where I had been staying with HER offspring, and their boys and girls. Can't say I missed them, except for White Eye, as they were a tad spineless for my taste. After that, I stayed with two-leg Kirsteen for a while. Couldn't understand why I was there, although SHE kept visiting me, and taking me out for rides. Eventually, SHE brought me back home here. Even this has changed a bit. My companion Vala has gone, and to be perfectly honest, I'm not sorry. If I - very rarely - feel the need for company of my own kind, I can always exchange a greeting with the biggish grey boy in the field just below. He's no conversationalist, being preoccupied with his next instalment of food, but it maintains polite relations. He does have a girl companion, but as she's of that very small, black and hairy type, which painful experience has proved to me to be prompt with teeth/hooves, I don't deign to dialogue with her. SHE is increasingly careful when moving around, these days, and because I don't have to compete for my forage any more, I've found it speeds the arrival of breakfast in my manger, if I stand aside, and allow HER to slither cautiously into place. Yes, many changes 'twixt last winter coat and this, but the comforting constant is carrot.

24. Peering Picasso

SHE trundled down by the light of the white thing that sometimes shines above at night. I was delighted, imagining that SHE'd chose to sacrifice some of HER rest times, in order to feed me extra-early. In recognition, I whinnied a greeting, but although SHE called a friendly reply, and HER horrid little meat-eater yapped inanely, SHE paused for only a moment to deposit the large object SHE'd been trundling, and return whence SHE'd come. As SHE trudged back up the track, I heard HER tell the meat-eater (who has the intellect of a dung-beetle) how glad SHE was to have remembered at the last minute, to put out the bin.

25. Picasso's Depilating

Even I am sceptical that my departing winter coat signals an improvement in the weather. SHE still has to break the cold, hard stuff which forms over my water bowl, every night.

At least it's dry, which has encouraged HER to give me a bit of a brushing. SHE's efficient at this, TBH, and knows where to go carefully, where to brush firmly so's not to irritate, and where to scour full steam ahead along the reaches of my back, which I can only access by rolling. SHE gleaned a very hairy harvest with each stroke, cleaning the brush regularly with another implement which does this job. Not far away, I heard Chuck and his mate chucking approvingly, in anticipation of pecking up fresh lining for their place. They also enjoy tidying up the seeds which fall as leftovers from my breakfast. We're a co-operative little community, hereabouts.

26. Praiseworthy Picasso

Phew, did I need a drink!

SHE bounded down, armed with carrot and halter. I accepted both, sighed and accompanied HER up the field. SHE paused twice for a breather, so I thoughtfully waited, admiring the view with HER. Finally brushed and saddled, I endured HER taking up HER place, though today SHE sat down with an unceremonious bump. Uncharacteristic, I admit, and SHE did apologise. A good day for a look around - bright and warm, with just enough light breeze to keep flies at bay. In gracious good humour, I walked and trotted as requested, even as far as entering that road I've refused to visit for ages.

Had a pit stop to trim someone's grass, whilst SHE chattered to its owner, then finally up the lovely grassy track, where we enjoy a canter. SHE advised caution, as some of those nasty prickly bushes lay on the path ahead, so being very canny, I slowed to walk carefully past them, to the next clear stretch. Whoopee! I cantered merrily along - SHE enjoys this as much as I do - and approached another bush lying in our way. Unfortunately, we had a tiny misunderstanding, in that I decided, in a fit of exuberance, to hop over it, SHE, clearly expecting me to circumnavigate. I jumped beautifully, but taken by surprise, SHE was badly left behind, and gave me another bump on my back. SHE was in a guddle - stirrup lost, clutching at my mane, begging me to stop (which I obediently did) till SHE sorted HERSELF out. I could tell that SHE thought I'd been very understanding, for SHE posted me down a morsel of carrot, then we resumed our route in a merry, uneventful canter.

Back home, SHE rubbed me down, then let me roll. I was glad of a cool, clean drink, and SHE always sees to it that I have plenty. However, of late, one of those flying creatures that hunts at night, making an extremely sinister noise into the bargain, has initiated the habit of eating its prey on the fence post beside my water bowl. Bad enough, yet it then hops onto the rim of the bowl, and poops in my drink! SHE has to empty and clean out this revolting mess every morning, for which I'm extremely grateful, in this hot weather, hence my co-operative mood.

27. Picasso's Pronouncement

I proudly pronounce that if you know, you know.

SHE brought me out of my field, which was very welcome, as it doesn't have much grass. I have no idea why SHE restricts my natural impulses to source ad-lib munching, but there it is.

I was allowed several opportunities to snatch some long, juicy mouthfuls, while being led up to HER home territory. After delivering a placatory pep-talk of some sort, SHE led me towards a strange new stable-thing, and requested me to follow HER up and in. Naturally, I refused point blank, and amused myself watching HER going in and out, several times, while I stood motionless. Bored soon, I introduced my intimidation tactic of snorting and pawing the ground. SHE ignored that, instead unsheathing a covered bucket I'd failed to notice. Never one to look a gift horse in the mouth, I placed one hoof on the approach ramp, whilst sniffing out the contents of the bucket. M'm...lovely fresh stuff, which I sampled and thoroughly enjoyed while walking up and into the box. Irritatingly, SHE made me follow the munching bucket in and out of the new place for a total of three times, before allowing me to enjoy the food in stationary mode. I have significant reserves of will power, but these are easily blocked by the lure of nourishment.

28. Picasso's Pleasure (and Pain)

A new day had hardly begun, when large moveable stables arrived, to halt by my field. I could hear the sounds of some of my kind, impatient to be let out, and bustled up to see what on earth was going on. There were lots of two-legs, bustling about opening up the stables, and SHE hurried down, to help them by opening the various gates. I recognised HER offspring, and the two grand foals who used to ride me, when I stayed with them. One of them led a big chestnut boy down, and into the field SHE'd opened for them. Next came a small bay boy......WHITE EYE!! I cantered right up to my fence, and called to him.

"Blue Eye?" He was being hurried past, so couldn't stop to talk just then, but was in fact just in the next bit of field, so we could see each other, touch noses even, but still had our own spaces. I was sorry about that from the point of being with White Eye, but there were three other boys - a handsome grey, and a jet black - who looked a tiny bit boisterous for my liking, so was relieved on the whole for a separating line of fencing. SHE had put out water for them, but they were all glad to run, stretch their legs and roll. I guessed that they had been travelling for a long time, as I had once done.

Once the two-legs had gone, taking their stables up to HER place, White Eye and I had a catch-up.

"I really missed you, you know." he said. "There's been quite a turnover of our kind, and I never got to know anyone very well. The new boy here (he indicated the chestnut) is OK, but still a bit of a kid."

"Who are the others?"

"Oh, they belong to the other two-legs. I often see them at events. They're OK too, but not pals, like you and me."

I nodded. "I'm on my own now, and actually prefer it, though," I added quickly, "It'd be different if you were here." A thought struck me. "Maybe you will stay here?"

"That'd be nice! Think I'm going to be busy, though I don't know what they've in mind."

White Eye was quite correct, in that very soon, all four were loaded up and away again, returning very much later in the day. I began to feel uneasy. Could it be that I too would shortly be loaded up and whisked away again. I asked White Eye if he knew anything, but he shook his head.

The next morning, there was a whirl of activity. The two-legs obviously wanted to go somewhere again, and White Eye decided that he didn't, evading capture with enviable dexterity. I had become more and more worried about all the unfamiliar activity round my normally peaceful place, and to cap it all, started to have a strange pain in my stomach. I tried to kick it away, and then tried lying down, to see if that would help, but it didn't. I groaned, and then the two-legs came to see what was the matter. In a very short time, SHE arrived, and spoke very kindly to me. SHE stood with me, doing HER best to rub my sore stomach gently, and soothed me while the other two-legs and their horses loaded up and went away.

"I hope you'll be alright, Blue Eye!" called White Eye.

"A gonner, for sure." commented the chestnut, callously.

SHE put on my halter, and led me slowly around, chatting away as SHE does. The pain in my stomach came and went, and I was glad that SHE was there. I accepted a peppermint, then I heard another thing arriving, and immediately a he-two-leg hurried in to see me. One of those types that looks into my mouth, and gives me the odd jab for no good reason. They took me into the stable, where I rarely go, and the he-two-leg stuck something against my stomach, resting his head almost on my side, listening for something. It was inevitable that I was to receive another jab, but was too preoccupied with my sore stomach to care much. After a few minutes, I was led outside again, and soon, the he-two-leg departed. SHE waited with me for a very long time, until I suddenly realised that I was feeling better. SHE had been very kind, and probably made my stomach better by rubbing it...or maybe it was that jab. Anyway, I decided that I'd been worrying about nothing. Of course I wasn't going to be sent away with all those boys. They were all obviously very good at doing whatever their two-legs wanted, whereas……..

29. Peripatetic Picasso

Trundled hither and thither yesterday. Ought to have realised that SHE intended to take me to one of those rather barbarous nag-fests which two-legs seem to favour, thinking about all the brushing, washing and spraying going on.

With the grey dawn, came HER offspring, to catch my dear old pal, White Eye (Ollie), from the adjacent field. I watched in amused approval, as he put on a sector-leading example of how to defy and evade a two-leg.

"Atta boy!" I snorted, as he sped past my fence, kicking up a defiant heel. He's a professional of course, so knows just how far he can go, before gracefully agreeing to be caught.

SHE arrived shortly, and placed some hay at what would clearly be our particular work-station. SHE was rather bemused that in spite of tactical overnight rugging, I'd indulged in a bout of tactical pooping, requiring emergency swabbing from my quarters. HER good friend Lorna arrived as usual, to help HER, and they were soon laughing and enjoying themselves. Peculiar creatures.

At the other workstations, there were varying degrees of tense preparation, both White Eye and the big chestnut boy returning slightly bad attitudes to their staff - an excess of unnecessary stamping and foozling about. I ignored them, concentrating on my brekkie. Finally my charges instructed me to climb into my new moving stable, so I stood politely at the foot of the ramp, till they remembered to offer me my food bucket, whereupon I clattered promptly up and in, as a role model for the others, especially White Eye, who was urging me, wickedly, to throw a wobbly.

What can I say about this herd event? Countless hoards of my kind, great and small. Flocks of tense two-legs, hyperventilating over goodness knows what. The grass was acceptable, so I went to work, until SHE obliged me to wear my saddle and bridle, which rather irritated me. I did allow HER access to my passenger deck, trying a gently intimidating bouncy pace, as advance warning against any expectations SHE might have had. SHE was insistent upon a collected walk past many of my kind. A bigger girl suddenly told me that she wanted to kick the living daylights out of me, and her two-leg obviously said as much to HER, so we beat a swift retreat from that threat. Ill mannered trollop of a creature.

SHE attempted to ride me into a warm-up ring. Naturally, being quite pleasantly warm already, I saw no need, and refused. Next followed the dismal chore of circling at a walk and trot, in the company of several others. They also did a fair bit of cantering, being servile creatures. SHE did try to have me follow suit, but a couple of advisory bucks from me acted as an effective deterrent. At last, the two-leg in charge (who, I perceived, took a rather dim view of my intelligent workload-management strategy) awarded HER a couple of inedible items - his assistant had already awarded me a peppermint - and we all exited.

No need to relate more of this outing. I was thoroughly glad to return home, roll most of the sprayed-on stuff off, have a drink and a relaxing lunch. You must remember that I'd had nothing so eat (between breakfast, hay in the trailer, grass at the event and more hay on the return journey) for the tedious time it took HER to remove my travel boots and tail guard before releasing me. Far too long.

30. Picasso's Parting

A fast or a feast. That's how it's seemed to me. First of all a total of four new boys arrived to stay next door to me. One of them was White Eye, which pleased us both very much, and the others kept themselves to themselves, which also suited us well.

Of course, the visiting two-legs, and there was quite a herd of them, were forever arriving with their moving stables, loading up the four boys, taking them away somewhere, and bringing them back later. I'd been rather upset about all this to begin with, even worrying myself into a sore stomach, as I told you, before it struck me that all the activity was nothing to do with me, and had no implications for my permanent residence here. One morning, the black and the grey boy were loaded up and taken away. White Eye and I had watched as they obediently followed their two-legs, offering no resistance.

"Spineless pair, if you ask me." White Eye was deeply critical. Suddenly the chestnut boy, who until then had offered nothing to our forum, started to gallop up and down the field, shrieking wildly that he'd lost his friends.

"You haven't lost your friends, saddo - 'cos you didn't have any!" White Eye can be cruelly cutting, when he chooses.

"Can I come over and talk to you?" The chestnut seemed to see me for the first time. "Ooh - one of your eyes is a funny colour! - Did you know that? - One of his eyes is a funny colour too! Ho, ho, ho!"

White Eye turned his heels towards the chestnut, who although still a very callow youth was nevertheless bright enough to understand genuine menace and galloped away, kicking up his heels when at a safe enough distance. We continued our reminiscences uninterrupted.

The following day it was very very wet, so much so that it was quite hard to see to the end of the fields. HER offspring and the grand foals arrived with their moveable stable.

"Oh no - going out again! I can't be bothered with them!" White Eye went into evasive mode, irritating his two-legs beyond belief, before ultimately allowing himself to be caught. The chestnut then decided that he was afraid of the stable thing, and stress levels escalated. At that point, both White Eye and I realised that we were about to be separated yet again. I watched him walk up the ramp first, giving a lead to the chestnut, then the door was raised and bolted. The chestnut's quarters showed

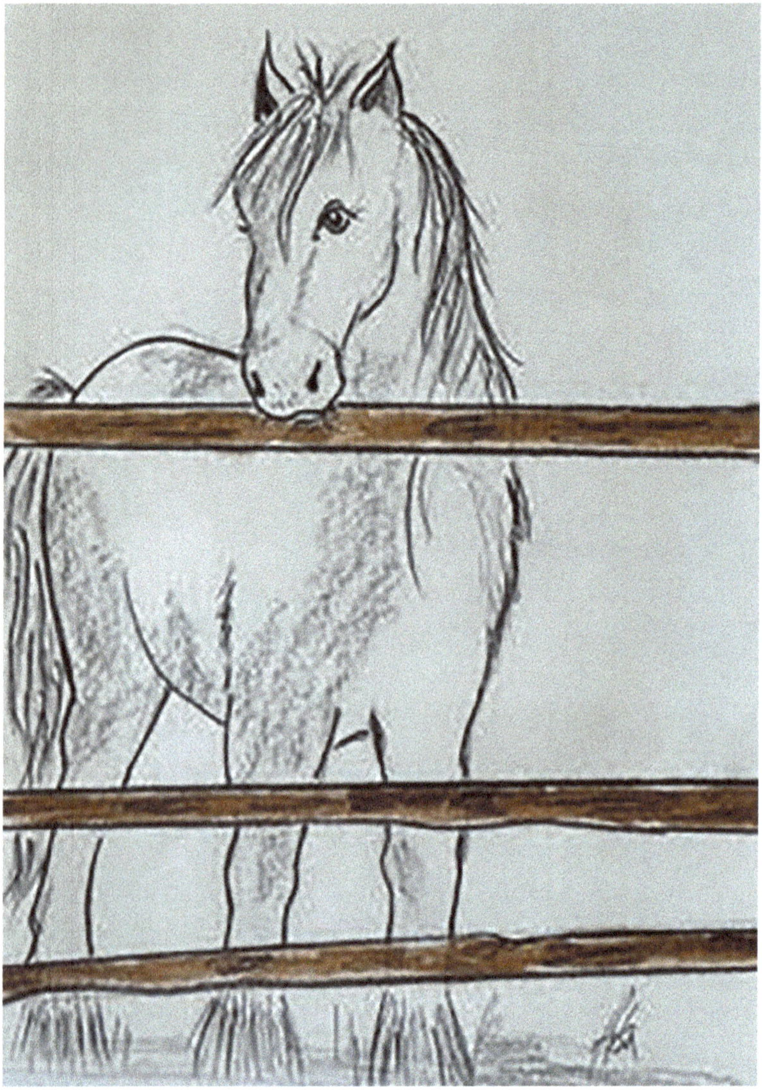

above the door, but White Eye was too small for me to see. I called to him.

"Where are you going?"

"I don't know! I don't want to leave you!"

The stable thing moved away slowly. I called frantically to White Eye, and tried to keep pace, but could only go as far as the boundary of my fence.

"White Eye - White Eye...come back!"

"I can't! Goodbye Blue Eye! Goodbye....."

His voice faded away along the road, until I couldn't hear anything except rain landing on the roof of my hay store. Sadly I stood on my own again, wondering if White Eye and I would ever have another brief encounter...or should it be encanter?

Milton Keynes UK
Ingram Content Group UK Ltd.
UKHW050415311024
450379UK00009B/154

9 781836 150411